I0640644

Charles Livingstone Stebbins

Harvard Lyrics and other Verses

Charles Livingstone Stebbins

Harvard Lyrics and other Verses

ISBN/EAN: 9783744769365

Printed in Europe, USA, Canada, Australia, Japan

Cover: Foto ©Andreas Hilbeck / pixelio.de

More available books at **www.hansebooks.com**

HARVARD LYRICS

And Other Verses

BEING SELECTIONS OF THE BEST VERSE
WRITTEN BY HARVARD UNDERGRADU-
ATES WITHIN THE LAST TEN YEARS

SELECTED BY

CHARLES LIVINGSTONE STEBBINS

OF THE CLASS OF NINETY-SEVEN

BOSTON

L. C. PAGE & COMPANY

MDCCCCI

Introduction

THE motive that prompted the compilation of this little volume was a desire to collect into convenient form some of the more serious thoughts of Harvard students as expressed in their best verse, with the hope of creating in the public mind a better impression of the standard of undergraduate literary work.

One would not claim for the poems here presented that they have the depth of a Browning or the metrical perfection of a Tennyson; but I believe one can assert with reason that they are worthy of the attention of thoughtful readers. Immature many of them may be, but all are indicative of serious mood and elevated purpose. This seriousness of student thought is too little recognized or understood by the outside world. The buoyant activity manifested in athletic and society life is practically the only side which the casual observer of student life knows. The deeper, more significant moods and aspirations of students are announced with no blare of trumpets.

One form of expression of these deeper feelings is college literature, and the strongest manifestation of this is verse. A student's philosophy of life as thus expressed is too often considered either superficial or

"sicklied o'er with the pale cast of thought,"

and thus in either case untrue to things as they are. In the former instance, he is believed superficial because he is a spectator only, and not yet an actor, in the drama of life; in the latter, morbid because ignorant — through inexperience — of the activity and the meaning of the great world that lies beyond the college gates. That there is superficiality and even childishness of thought on the one hand, and narrowness and morbidness on the other, cannot be denied; but that such mental conditions are necessarily college characteristics, or in any true sense typical of the better undergraduate thought, this collection of verse seems to me to disprove. University life in these modern days is not that of monastic seclusion, but that of the broad, true culture which springs from sympathetic contact with the best in the world about us.

If, then, this collection of verse gives evidence of some rational interpretation of human life, evidence that our most thoughtful students are actuated by high ideals, the purpose of this book will have been accomplished.

I wish to express my thanks to the Editors of the HARVARD ADVOCATE and the HARVARD MONTHLY for the privilege of making selections from those periodicals; to Messrs. Copeland and Day for permission to use copyrighted verse of Mr. Bates and Mr. Savage; and to Mr. F. W. C. Hersey, whose excellent literary judgment has been of much assistance to me in preparing this compilation.

C. L. S.

CAMBRIDGE, MASS.,
March, 1899.

Contents

𝔓art I

Contents

Contents

Part II

Part I

Miscellaneous Verse

Harvard Lyrics

AD PARNASSUM

UNPEOPLED plains lie in the smoky west;
   Child of the evening earth, a traveller I
   Pace onward silent where the shadows die
In the vast mountain of my distant quest.
This Occident, with strangeness ever blessed,
   Pervades the vision of the inward eye,
   And, whispering of some nobler destiny,
Leads from the tangled paths by man possessed.
Out of the tents, out of the hearts of men,
   Unwearied fled I one forgotten morn;
I left no word, I asked no right to ken
   The joy and pain behind me daily borne.
I shall some evening gain my height, and then
   Survey the universe before the dawn.

ROBERT STEED DUNN, '98

IN A COPY OF THE "VITA NUOVA"

HALF-CONSCIOUS here the master lays
  His fingers on the lyre;
Sweet, simple, strong, the notes he plays, —
Notes that have tuned for years and days
  The soul's devotion higher.

Unwitting of his noble might,
  In steadfast faith he sings,
Telling the way to find aright,
In Love's clear, calm, unflickering light,
  Life's best, divinest things.

RUSSELL HILLIARD LOINES, Sp.

THE LOVE TIDE

I BUILT a house upon the shifting strand,
  Moulding with childish hands a rough design,
  All heedless of the tremulous silver line
Where came the water nibbling up the sand
Until it touched me, bubbling o'er my hand,
  And melting down those parapets of mine.
  I checked the tears, and saw the low sun shine
Red o'er the blue, and tried to understand.

What were the toys that love came knocking o'er
  Ere I had seen the flood of life he brought?
  His tide washed out the treasures I had sought
And laid my sand-heaps level with the shore.
  Lo, a blue sea with golden sunlight fraught
Surged where a little mound had been before.

JOHN ALBERT MACY, '99.

"METHINKS THE MEASURE"

METHINKS the measure of a man is not
    To save a state in midst of fierce alarms,
    Do noble deeds and mighty feats of arms,
And feel the breath of battle waxing hot.
There have been Cæsars whose more humble lot
    Forbade that they should bear the victor's
        palms;
    Cromwells who never left their peaceful farms;
Napoleons without ambition's blot.

Not in the deed that's done before the eyes
    Of wonder-stricken lands upturned to view,
But in the will, though no occasion rise,
    And sleeping still, that dares such deeds to do,
Is drawn the line which parts him from the clods
And gives a man a kinship with the gods.

                    PERCY ADAMS HUTCHISON, '99.

FROM A WINDOW

THROUGH dusky etchings of the wood
    The white snows glow,
The tree arms, twined in sisterhood,
    Together grow.
    Brown grasses dead
  Beside the tree-trunks lie;
    Clear overhead
Bends down the tender sky,
And in my heart, O friend, a thought of thee! —
O world of God, thou art so dear to me!

CHARLES T. SEMPERS, '88.

2

A PLACE TO WORSHIP TRUTH

I LOVE that spot upon the hill, the place
Where we have often sat the twilight through,
Where lovely dreams were built in summer's sky,
And we forgot life's cares in revery.
To add by distance still another charm,
And make more sweet that dear, secluded spot,
Far down below the busy World was seen
By glimmering lamp, and heard by tolling bell.
Yes, a place well chosen to tell our dreams of love,
To speak of God, and fathom what we could
Of that great Force which governs all that is, —
A spirit world, because we felt and said
Just what the mind when free is wont to think;
A place to feel and know and worship Truth.

C. H. M.

TO PAN

O PAN, come back; our age hath need of thee;
We have forgot the beauty of the fields.
And though, in thy time, every nook and tree
Could give some message to the lords of earth,
Our ears hear naught; and as each object yields
Unto us gold we estimate its worth.
We have forgot the secret of the sea;
And though we count the very grains of sand
As they fall glistening from our open hand,
We may not know what they could tell to thee.

O Pan, come back! and teach to us the tongue
All nature spoke in thy far golden days;
For all things spoke then, and the world was
    young,
But now we cannot hear the piteous words
Wherewith the pent-up forest-spirit prays
For mercy when we fell her tree.   The birds
Sing senseless songs unto our senseless ears.
We heed them not; or if by chance we heed,
'T is but to slay them, giving them a meed
Which would have filled thy kindly eyes with
    tears.

O Pan, come back! or if thou canst not come,
Send us a message from the over world.
Nay, wilt thou speak not, be forever dumb?
Can we know nothing of the frank delight
Wherewith men lived their life ere they were
    hurled
Unto dark doubt from out thy trusting light?
Nay, thou art gone, we know it; death's stern rod
Hath smitten thee who had no thought of death.
Thy mighty limbs were vain, and vain the breath
Which piped and made men glad once, poor, dead
    god!

HUGH McCULLOCH, JR., '91.

"LEST WE FORGET!"

LORD of the Living, in Whose sight
  A thousand years are Yesterday
Or as the watches of the night,
  Show Living Man the Living Way!

The world doth clamor at our gate,
  The world's huge hunger goes unfed;
Shall sable gown be more than meat,
  Or crust of culture more than bread?

Immurèd in the cloistral cell
  We hear the unfettered eagles cry!
Our beads of learning we o'ertell,
  And dawn draws dragons in the sky!

Lord Captain Christ, Whose morning-eyne
  Are stars that shall not brook control,
Renew the Primitive Design,
  Rebreathe in Man a Living Soul!

FULLERTON W. WALDO, '98.

DUSK

THE maid sits by the spinning-wheel,
  With head bowed low in dreaming,
And looks not where the shadows steal
  Or dusk's lone star is gleaming.

The tremulous wheel stirs into rest;
  Clasped lightly are her fingers;
And only in her swelling breast
  A pulse of movement lingers.

Through casement dim a faint wind drifts,
  Since morn asleep 'mid roses;
The yellow hair it lightly lifts
  That on her cheek reposes.

A bird is singing far away,
  Beyond the upland meadows,
One late clear song across the gray
  And drowsy world of shadows.

Ah! vain the wind of twilight stirs,
  Sings thrush from distant cover.
She hears not them, but moaning firs
  That darken o'er her lover.

And all unwatched the shadows steal,
So fast her tears are gleaming, —
Dear maid beside the spinning-wheel,
With head bowed low in dreaming.

B. F. GRIFFIN, '99.

ZOË

DOWN by the rocks of old Ocean,
  When the sun stole slowly to die,
Leaving a purple remembrance
  Illumined with gold in the sky;
Bathed in the flood of the twilight,
  Where the waves were lapping the shore,
Leaping in ridges and running
  High beachward with hiss and with roar; —
Cushioned 'mid driftweed and pebbles,
  Sat Zoë, and gazed o'er the tide, —
Rapt as the Magdalen weeping
  Had mused on Him that had died.

Thought flooded soul, and a longing, —
  As if life were not all it seems,
Incomplete somehow or somewhere,
  Fantastic and flitting as dreams;
Longing to know all the *un*known, —
  For the known is grievously brief, —
Those things that mortals must *not* know,
  But must work and live in belief.

Trembling with each crowded pulse-beat,
  She yearned for hope's guerdon, — love's sigh ;
Only gray faces of memory
  Dimly clustered in answer star-high.
Slowly her tears brimming hotly
  ·Plashed down like raindrops at een ;
Sob on sob, heartwrung in bursting,
  Died low o'er the water's cold sheen.

Tramping through gloom of black shadows,
  Hard-muscled, grim Toil strode that way,
Spied he the sick o' the heart's ache
  And kissed, ere the night paled to gray ;
Thrilled her slow blood by his touching,
  By brave songs of work, till her grief
Floated adown streams of Lethe
  Like a dusky, tide-swept leaf.

FRANK W. C. HERSEY, '99.

AN APRIL NIGHT

ACROSS the risen moon dark banks of clouds
  In flying scuds and vapory masses sweep.
  They dull in brilliancy, but cannot keep
Some light from rifting through their fleecy
    shrouds.
Below, the sleeping earth, in fitful chase
  Of changing lights and shadows, sometimes lies
  Bathed in a silvery radiance, when the skies
Allow the struggling moon to show its face;
But oftener wrapped in darkness it remains.
    The rushing night-winds sweeping through the
      trees,
    The noise of waters on their rocky bed,
Alone disturb the silent calm that reigns
  O'er hills and valleys, woods and fertile leas.
    The living world is quiet as the dead.

HARRISON J. HOLT, '98.

LOVE'S PRAYER

LOVE, like Religion, has its prayer:
  " Give me this day my daily bread."
Poor Love, that has so much to bear,
  So seldom is its hunger fed.
It asks for loaves: instead there come,
In answer, only crust and crumb,
And often, as it pleads alone,
It gains no other bread than stone.

And still it breathes this simple want;
  Alas! it knows no other prayer;
Nor ease can lure, nor failure daunt,
  Nor terrors drive it from its care.
Deceived so oft, wouldst thou not guess
'T would faint for very weariness?
Nay, it will plead till prayer be dead,
" Give me this day my daily bread ! "

FREDERIC LAWRENCE KNOWLES, '96.

VITA MEA

WITH fear I trembled in the House of Life,
  Hast'ning from door to door, from room to
    room,
  Seeking a way from that impenetrable gloom
Against whose walls my strength lay weak from
    strife.
All dark! All dark! And what sweet wind was
    rife
  With earth, or sea, or star, or new sun's bloom,
  Lay sick and dead within the place of doom,
Where I went raving like the winter's wife.

"In vain, in vain!" with bitter lips I cried;
"In vain, in vain!" along the hallways died
  And sank in silences away. Oppressed,
I wept. Lo! through those tears the window-
    bars
Shone bright, where Faith and Hope like long-
    sought stars
  First gleamed upon that prison of unrest.

W. STEVENS, Sp.

LONG AGO

COME, Harrietta, shadows fall
  Across the hill: 'tis eventide.
  They stretch their figures far and wide;
And from the moor the crickets call.
The night moves on: the sunset glow
  Fades down into the dusky air;
  I seem to see that glory there
That thrilled my being long ago.

There is the river stealing by;
  How still it looks, how dark and deep!
  As though a grim and lasting sleep
Had fallen from the starless sky.
Slow as the stream my dull thoughts flow
  Adown the channel of the years,
  Clogged with the sorrows and the tears
That pressed upon me long ago.

Do you remember when we stood
  One autumn eve, when leaves were red,
  And sunset purple glory shed
Aslant the caverns of the wood?

I saw your gentle head bent low,
    Your drooping eyes; my heart beat fast;
    I tried to speak; the moment passed, —
And so I lost you long ago.

We talked, I think, of common things;
    I have forgotten what they were, —
    Of harvest time, of him and her,
In that forced tone that error brings.
'T was dark, and with a genial glow
    The old house cast a merry light
    That seemed to cheer the gloomy night,
But left me cheerless long ago.

Time flies and leaves an empty place;
    We toil and struggle as we can,
    Live out our lives to plot and plan
For high resolve or deep disgrace.
We learn our failings; learn to know
    The good and ill that in us lies;
    We hold the mirror to our eyes
And see the faults of long ago.

I seek not more; the past is dead;
    Its mask is left on you and me.
    We are not what we sought to be, —
Our dreams are gone, our visions fled.

Let age her mantle round us throw.
  I have no secret now from you :
  My heart is yours as firm and true
As by the woodland long ago.

PERCY LOUIS SHAW, '97.

TO KEATS

Asleep, awake, in dreams of poesy
And all the lambent joys of Arcady,
  He found a faun once, sleeping in a dell,
  Far from the noon's fierce heat, 'neath poppy'd
    spell.
He struck the old Greek chord of sympathy
With woods and streams, all nature's minstrelsy,
  And knew the moon's pale splendors. He
    could tell
  Where wood-nymphs drowse in dales of aspho-
    del —
Ah! Keats, we mourn thee. In our hearts the
    pain
  Of thy young life yet lives. We have no tears;
  Dry-eyed, expectant still, each dawn appears.
But many springs may dawn, and many wane,
  Ere Earth, old Earth, prosaic through the years
That thou art gone, shall deck herself again.

GEORGE GRISWOLD, 2d, '93.

ON SEEING MONADNOCK MOUNTAIN

AFTER READING EMERSON'S POEM

MONADNOCK! Solitary mountain! I
  Behold at last thy grand and lonely peak
  Staying the driving cloud, as thou didst seek
To hold communion with the bending sky.
About thy base the lesser hill-tops lie,
  But not at hand, as if they felt how weak
  Were they by thee who in the past didst speak
Of God to hearts which reverently drew nigh.

And to one other didst thou speak of God,
  One who did hold thee as a friend, and dear;
  Who, prophet, poet, and a leader seer,
Holding within his hand stern Moses' rod,
  Arose, like thee, above each lesser height,
  And earth and sky beheld with undimmed sight.

PERCY ADAMS HUTCHISON, '99.

3

BEFORE THE BATTLE

"TO-NIGHT," they said,
 "When the day is dead,
When we are slain, or the foe is fled;
   At set of sun,
   When all is done,
When all is lost, or the fight is won, —
   Then we shall sleep
   In Death's dark keep,
Or drink red wine till the night is deep.
   Ride! Ride!
   With our wrath to guide,
   Into the battle, sword by side!

   "To-night," they laughed,
   As they stooped and quaffed
The red fierce wine from the stirrup-cup,
   "To-night, when we come
   The funeral drum
Shall throb, to startle their hearts that sup,
   Or the flags shall stream
   And the banners gleam,

And the trumpets blow triumph as we ride up !
>   Ride !   Ride !
>   With our wrath to guide,
>   Into the battle, sword by side !

>   " Away, and away,
>   For the morn is gray
And the sword-blades hunger and stir in the
>   sheath,
>   And above the hills
>   The red sky fills
With the dawning terror of blood beneath ;
>   The white blades burn
>   And the keen spears yearn
To harvest the red ripe field of Death.
>   Ride !   Ride !
>   With our wrath to guide,
>   Into the battle, sword by side ! "

HERBERT BATES, '90.

THE MANSE AT CONCORD

APART from traffic of the world, in shroud
   Of moaning pines and solemn ash-trees tall,
   Where throbbing notes of red-breasts rise
      and fall,
Green-mossèd stands the Manse, — gray grown,
      and proud
Of ancient days.   Here priestly sires have bowed,
   And priestly sons, in meek prayer pastoral.
   When quivering lip sang out the righteous
      call
Each window shivered 'mid the battle-cloud.
Here trod the brooding, dark-eyed Puritan;
   The soulful Scholar closed his yellow tome,
Spake forth, an haloed Sage, to wakening man;
   The Patriot marched with gown and book
      from home.
   Now, hushed as creeps yon dusky stream, the
      tide
Of years flows o'er the Mansion glorified.

FRANK W. C. HERSEY, '99.

THE PLACE OF LOVE

LOVE, thou art not alone for gentle dells,
Where summer breezes, sweetly perfumed, breathe
     Through heavy branches
Thy place is also where the winter wind
Roars down the long, bleak hill;
     The flying snow
Doth blind the traveller, as he strives to gain
The little cottage under sheltering pines,
     Where thou art waiting, Love.

S. C. BRACKETT, '91.

MEMORIAL TOWER

THE whole world drowses in the quiet power
    Of summer moonlight. City, village, farm,—
    All common things are sunk beneath the
        charm;
And dreams of the immortal throng the hour.
And lo, mute witness of our life, yon tower
    Rises to heaven in a nightly tryst;
    White, like a phantom folded in the mist,
As if it had eternity for dower.
And thus at last when all the froth of strife
    Is long subsided in the wake of time,
      And we are fled like billows on the sea,
Immortal moonlight shall recall our life,
    And with its silver sheen like winter rime
      Shall merge our memories with eternity.

JOHN R. CORBIN, '92.

THE SECRET

I WANDERED with my flute through the
  forest,
  And played to the hearkening birds.
I played them a secret, sweet and soft,
  Too sweet for the jargon of words.
It arose like a delicate perfume
  To the tree-tops up in the sky,
While all the marvelling songster-choir
  Sat hushed in the boughs on high.

For I sang of a night in the garden
  When a wondrous gliding Dream
Allured me along, — like a shallop afloat
  On a slow-descending stream, —
Through the pathways dim in the darkness,
  Far down by orchards and bowers,
To the Favored Vales, inwoven thick
  With numberless growing flowers.

'T was the form of a matchless maiden;
  One hand held a lily-bloom;
In its chalice a Lamp of golden fire
  That shone through the misty gloom.

" This is what men are seeking,"
  She seemed to be singing afar,
Uplifting the snow-white lily-bloom,
  All alight with the rose-red star.

" In the heart of this beautiful flower
  Truth has written his name.
Blest the possessor ! " — I clasped the prize
  As an infant clasps a flame.
But then the bright Vision vanished ;
  A night-bell smote the air ;
And I stood alone in the garden dark
  On the pathway bleak and bare.

All around me the numberless blossoms
  Danced with a cheerless mirth.
I looked in their hearts for the heavenly Light
  That never was seen on earth.
And I saw in the heart of a lily
  Some faintest trace remain
Of the Light men seek in their own dim hearts
  And the world's wide heart in vain.
    .   .   .   .

I have marred the soft, sweet secret
  In the rude, cold speech of man.
It bubbled away like a laugh of joy
  In the shade of the woodlands wan.

But, alas! the poor dreamer is tongueless,
  Nor can bare his soul in words;
He wanders with his flute through the forest
  calm,
  And plays to the hearkening birds.

WILLIAM A. LEAHY, '88.

THE COMING OF THE STORM

WHAT darkens in the west?
  (Hark, how the gulls are calling!)
The spread black hand of the storm
  That grows with the twilight's falling.

What gathers in the east?
  (Hark, how the beaches rattle!)
The march of the columned clouds
  That gather to the battle.

Dark and slow, row on row,
  The ranks of the east assemble,
And under their line the sea's ranks shine,
  And the long shores quake and tremble.

The swift scud streams, the white foam gleams,
  And fierce shall the onset be;
And God be his help that strives to-night
  With the armies of the sea.

Black ridges with white, mad manes,
  Beaches that roar and rattle,
And a wind that ranges the wild sea-line,
  Driving the waves to battle.

HERBERT BATES, '90.

CHRIST CHURCH

OLD wooden church, with tower square and
  low, —
Playground and graveyard meeting at thy gate, —
Standing these hundred years inviolate,
Alone unmoved amid the world's swift flow;
Beneath thy shade the playful children grow,
And youths, in silent prayer, oft contemplate
The sober thoughts thy cross or chimes relate:
How God is real within this world of show;
All else hath changed since men first raised thy
    walls,
But through the fleeting years, unaltered still,
Its message to mankind thy presence gives;
The truth to minds of all who pass recalls
That time destroys all works of human skill,
And God, alone unchanged, eternal lives.

CHAUNCEY II. BLODGETT, '92.

WHEN DARKNESS FALLS

IF this be sleep,
Sit by me while I sleep; if this be death,
No mortal power may stay the fading breath;
But stay thou by me, be it sleep or death.

If this be sleep,
When I awake, I fain would see thee by.
Watch thou my bed with thine unsleeping eye,
And take my hand in thine when I awake.

If this be death,
Speed thou my soul upon thy steady prayer;
If this be death, I go I know not where.
Oh, stay thou by me, be it sleep or death.

ROBERT PALFREY UTTER, '98.

EASTER MORNING

I WAITED for the day with anxious dread;
" Shall darkness triumph o'er the light?" I said;
But as I spoke the solemn silence thrilled
With joyous song that night's vast portals filled.

The depths of gloom denied the coming morn.
My soul was sick with fear till day was born.
But when from eastern bondage burst the sun,
I felt within that victory was won.

The sterile air grew rich with heaven-sent lays;
They filled my heart, that almost burst with praise,
For then I knew the bitter days were past;
I saw the triumph of the light at last!

J. D. BARRY, '88.

TO GERTRUDE

THOU standest upon the threshold of the day,
   Still dancing in the sunlight of the morn ;
   Thy sky is clear, the blue of it untorn
By any cloud of past or future gray.
Thy childhood plucks thee back, thy hopes away
   To the green distance of thy fancy born ;
   Thy laughs are long, thy sorrow quickly shorn, —
Thou art an April peeping into May.

So be thou ever ! Twine thy childish past
   Of simple thought so strongly to each thought
Of now and of to-morrow, that thou hast
A life unbroken, e'en a daisy chain,
   Binding thy was, thy is, thy shall, self-wrought,
Ever to lead thee back and on again.

EDWARD G. KNOBLAUCH, '96.

SAILOR'S REQUIEM

WRAP him in his hammock shroud;
  Heavy shotted let it be.
Gently lift him overside,
  Lower to the waiting sea.

Alike to him are listless calm
  And the fiercest storm that blows;
Southern, fever-dealing suns,
  Northern seas of ice and snows.

Never shall the vexing waves
  Waken him again from sleep,
Sinking, sinking slowly down,
  Through the dayless, nightless deep.

Mourn him not as one that's lost;
  He was cradled by the wave;
Home for him was on the sea,
  And the sea should be his grave.

PERCY ADAMS HUTCHISON, '99.

EFFORT

THE way is steep; high hangs the laurel
    wreath;
    It is the height that makes it worth the try.
    What boots attainment? In the striving lie
The sole rewards. Fight onward with set teeth !
Though swift the treadmill ground may slip
    beneath,
    Fight on ! Thy blows have paid thee as they
    fly;
    They have been dealt, and that must satisfy.
Then let thy sword be stranger to its sheath !

Though 'neath the rainbow's tip no treasure-pot
    Shall flash its golden welcome at the last,
    When from the sky the phantom long has
    passed,
When the vain dreams that led thee are forgot,
    Across a chasm men's sons shall look aghast,
And say, " He leapt this," — and shall mark the
    spot.

JOHN ALBERT MACY, '99.

A SEA DREAM

THE summer sunset sheds its glow
  Upon the changing sea;
The surging waters ebb and flow
  And bear their song to me.

And far away, against the sky,
  Their white sails listless spread,
The stately ships move slowly by
  Across the sunset red.

I love to watch at eventide
  The evanescent fires
That light the cloudland far and wide
  With minarets and spires;

To hear the dark, deep billows roll
  And break upon the shore,
To feel their echo in the soul
  That throbs their burden o'er.

For then the world grows dim and high,
  Those nobler fancies rise
That bear me toward that hidden sky
  Where love and duty lies.

4

I cross the threshold of the night
   In gems of glory wrought;
The stars pale in the wondrous light
   Sprung from the depths of thought.

The wind sighs on the sullen sea;
   My vision fades to air.
The clouds break wide with motion free,
   And peace is everywhere.

PERCY LOUIS SHAW, '97.

MY HERITAGE

I WOULD dwell in stately halls
  Where my fathers dwelt before;
But the house where the poor man lived
  Is known to earth no more.
I would walk the selfsame streets
  Where my fathers once were known;
But the path which the wanderer trod
  Has no memorial stone.
But I read the grand old books,
  And dream the grand old dreams,
, Till the beauty of life flashes out
  And illumines my path with its beams.
These books are the stately halls
  Which my fathers once possessed,
And the heritage I hold
  Is the dream within my breast!

RAYMOND L. WEEKS, '90.

LOVE IN TWILIGHT

My love is like an even star,
   Sweet glory in a purple gloaming.
No spangled gem, no golden spar
My love is; like an even star, —
An hope to heal when doubts do mar,
   And guerdon of a long day's roaming.
My love is like an even star,
   Sweet glory in a purple gloaming.

F. W. C. HERSEY, '99.

THE VOICE OF THE WEST WIND

THE Wind of the East and the Wind of the
    North
From the gates of the Sun and the Cold blow
    forth;
They wander wide and they wander free,
But never a word do they speak to me.
I hear but the voice I know the best,
Of my brother-in-blood, the Wind of the West;
And the word that the West Wind whispers
    me
Is a message, Heart of my heart, for thee.

Heart of my heart, when the skies hang low,
And all day long the light winds blow,
When the South, and the East, and the North
    are gray,
And the soft rain falls through the autumn day,
Then, Light of my soul, canst thou not hear
The voice of the West Wind, soft and clear?

" Come," he whispers, and " Come," again,
Leave the dull skies and the steady rain,
Leave thou the lowlands and chill gray sea,
Heart of my own heart, and come with me.

ROBERT PALFREY UTTER, '98.

AT DAWN

THE burden of the slaying of a king:
One hour he woke before the day-dawning,
And saw the faint sky whiten and the torn
Rack of the storm across the front of morn,
And he alone in darkness; for his bride,
New-wed at eve, was vanished from his side
And all the house in silence as of death.
Then wakened sudden as the wind's great breath
A sound of swift feet hurrying, — flashing swords
In the dim doorways; eyes of angry lords
Silent and stern for slaying. And she stood
Midmost among them, clad in red like blood
And gold as flame for burning, with keen eyes
Cold as the portals of the pale sunrise;
Nor any spoke a word, but, one by one,
They strode unto him, and the deed was done
Swift, silent as God's vengeance. Last, she came
And stood by him, and spoke one single name,
Her lover's, slain at eve by his command.
Then with one stately motion of her hand

She bade them thence, and followed, leaving there
The dead king lying, all his uncrowned hair
Moist from the blood of many wounds yet warm,
While all the dawn roared with the rising storm.

HERBERT BATES, '90.

ROSES

ON the beach she lingered idly,
　　'Neath the mossy headland's lee,
Looking out across the water.
　　Ah, but she was fair to see;
Roses nestled in her hair,
　　" Red for him and white for me."

When the last farewell was spoken
　　These the parting words he said:
" Meet me at the shore returning;
　　Wear the roses on your head
'Mid your bonny raven tresses,
　　White for you, for me the red."

Day by day the summer lengthened,
　　Faded into autumn drear;
Day by day, bedecked with roses,
　　Waited still the maiden here,
Till at last hope died within her
　　And she ceased to watch and fear.

Spring was redolent with blossoms
As they bore her to the sea,
And to rest they gently laid her
'Neath the mossy headland's lee;
On her grave they planted roses,
" Red for him and white for me."

C. HUNNEMAN, '89.

THE GULL

THE wild-eyed, savage gull with bowed wing
    tips
The white, flat surface of the misty sea;
Or stooping in the wind-trod, hollow wave
Reels upward straight, hangs quivering, his whole
    self
Intent, and breaks the surface like a bolt.
This spirit of the ocean mystery
Sweeps by in silence on the noisy scud,
Or cuts across the borders of the storm,
A flash of horrid white; with beating wings
Struggles in futile, royal wrath against
The armed battalions of a mighty wind,
And beaten, leaps aloft upon the storm
To ride in fury down the conquering gale.
Away, thou symbol of my own gray thoughts!
Whenever from the heaven of weary hopes
The clouds run low in the palely flowing sky;
Whenever from the world of the unachieved
The mists mount up to meet the drooping cloud,
And I between them fail, — 't is thou I see,

Thou dreadful emblem of my darker life.
Thou art no child of sunlight, for indeed,
Whether beneath some purple summer eve
Thou weariest thy way into the west,
Or in the winter on the frozen bay
Standest erect, a white, mad, ravened king,
Life-banished by the ice, thou art the same,
Grim, busy with thyself, hard, gloomy, wild.

P. H. SAVAGE, '93.

THE LOST PLEIAD

O THOU, who from the happy realms and
    bright
  Hast vanished into traceless depths and dark,
  Where none thy dread and icy path may mark
Amid the boundless terrors of the night;
Wherefore has God sent on thee such drear
    blight?
  Poor star, o'ershadowed as a hopeless heart;
  Poor star, unheeded as a broken dart,
That spent unwatched astray its destined flight.
Nay, rather, as some arrow of the chase,
  From God's sure hand thou cam'st, and now
    again
He sends thee where no hope thy path may
    trace,
  In sad and cold eclipse awhile, and then
    Maybe he shall recall thee to our sight,
    To shine at last forever in his light.

H. S. SANFORD, '88.

O MY BELOVED

I

A HUNGER infinite doth cry
　　From out my empty soul for thee;
Thy love alone can satisfy
　　The aching want that tortures me
　　And wastes my life in poverty.

O my Belovèd, I had thought
　　By many a path to come to thee;
Through wanderings weary I have sought
　　To find thy home, where it may be,
　　And in thine heart my name to see.

I wander lonely in the night,
　　I shiver naked in the cold;
Thy love my shelter is and light.
　　O God! my suppliant hands behold
　　The while my eager prayer is told.

I pray, Belovèd, not for days
　　Unmeasured by the ageless sun,
But on life's sea of warring ways

To know thy holy will is done,
And every fight for thee is won.

Then joy! To rest in thy great soul,
To know my life divine must be,
And as thy full waves o'er me roll
With flood of peace or misery,
To know, O God, they come from thee.

So, soft to die, and in thy love
To rest as on th' embosoming sea,
With nothing round, below, above,
But thy great heart enfolding me,
And so to sleep eternally.

O my Belovèd, not for bliss
Of endless life in worlds to be,
Nor yet for earthly joy in this
My heart most hungers, but for thee,
Whose love alone is life to me.

Yet it were sweet, O Love Divine,
At dawn of fresh eternity
To feel thy life enfolding mine,
To wake from death, immortal, free,
And lose yet find myself in thee.

II

O Love ! O Life ! So near thou art
　　I need not seek afar for thee,
Lo, in the pantings of my heart,
　　Thy present spirit gives to me
　　Thy love — for long eternity !

CHARLES T. SEMPERS, '88.

CONTRAST

STRANGE mingling here of laughter and of
      tears,
Of light and shade, of sunshine and of rain,
Of love and trust, and falterings and fears,
Of rue and heartsease, pleasure and of pain.
The greening blade cradles the yellow leaf,
The earth lies brown and warm beneath the snow;
Bright joy is nurtured in the lap of grief,
Swiftly our sorrows come and swiftly go.
We stand a moment on this changing verge,
This little rim of brightness, set between
The unknown, darksome wastes. One rising surge,
Then we pass on, from unseen to unseen,
Out of the night, o'ershadowing the To-Be,
Into the morning of Eternity.

                              SEVER B. BUCK, '98.

"IN MEMORIAM"

TO-NIGHT, when chill winds tear away
   From shivering bough the pallid leaf,
   I think of him who sang in grief,
"Our little systems have their day;

"They have their day and cease to be."
   He is not dead, but aye shall give
   Pure, tuneful solace; he shall live,
The beacon of a century.

GEORGE PHILBROOK, '94.

TO A TRAVELLER

SOME hearts there are that see afar
  The goal toward which they wend;
Some souls have sight to mark the light
  That shows the journey's end;
But some must still strive to fulfil
  What each day sets before,
Content to find there waits behind
  Each task a duty more.

And who shall say that knows the way,
  That those who travel slow
May not win much that passes such
  As see where they shall go?
Perhaps there lies another prize
  That may outshine this star,
And he who waits may know the Fates
  And see them as they are.

                    RUPERT S. HOLLAND, 1900.

THE SONG OF THE SAILOR'S DEATH

OH, the canny, canny landsman,
  When the wind howls loud, says he:
" 'T is good to abide at your own hearth-
    side
  When the storm is on the sea."

And the wandering sailor's canny wife
  With the bairns about her knee,
Says, " Would your daddy were safe at home,
  When the storm is on the sea."

But man must die; and so, say I,
  What use to bide at home?
There 's danger there as sure and sair
  As on the deep sea foam.

'T is dull to die an idle death,
  And, waste with misery,
For days in bed to lie as dead,
  E'er the suffering soul pass free.

Give me to die on the salt, salt sea,
  And go, like a sailor brave,
On the gale to my death by God's own breath,
  To a deep and unmarked grave.

Give me to go with the gale in my teeth,
  Down to my tossing grave ;
When his hour is come, at sea or home,
  No power a man can save.

And it needs not to sing me the Passing Song,
  It needs not to greet for me ;
The God of Heaven shall speed my soul,
  For He broodeth on the sea.

                    ROBERT PALFREY UTTER, '98.

STORM SONG

WHEN the bar with surf is ringing,
　And the seas are pitching high;
When the gull the wave is winging,
　And the gray clouds sheet the sky, —

Then the drowned men chant their dirges,
　Risen from their restless sleep;
Then they toss between the surges;
　Then they whistle o'er the deep.

Storm-beat sailors, homeward crawling,
　See a face they long thought dead,
Hear a dead man calling, calling,
　See his weed-entangled head.

Such a night Death's spell is blighted,
　And his prisoners all set free.
Then they dance, by watch-fire lighted;
　Then they howl, and roam the sea.

CLARENCE S. HARPER, Sp.

A FRIEND

THY face, my friend, is graven on my heart,
Traced by the finger of that Wingless Love
That draws a man unto his friend with bonds
Not lightly to be sundered.
                                    Still I sit
Beneath the single lamp's well-tempered glow;
I hear the roaring of the tameless night,
The rattle of the unencountered latch,
But thou art gone.   Thy place beneath our lamp
Is empty; and my life is empty, too.
Men come and go, and for some little space
They call me, friend, unweening what they say;
But thou art gone, and still I sit alone.
The book slips from my hand, and to mine eyes,
Weary and dim with pages turned in vain,
A vision rises of thy kindly face
Smiling with tranquil strength into my face.
My heart is filled with a strange sense of hope,
My hand goes forth to touch thee.
                                    Thou art gone.

The small, sharp crackling of thine empty chair
Brings back the cruel sense of loneliness,
For thou art gone indeed, and I alone
Must bear my burden to the hopeless end.

GAILLARD THOMAS LAPSLEY, '93

FUTURITY

LIKE the reflection on the window-glass
Of scenes and objects which around us pass,
The present seems; while through its image dim
Night, like the future, forms one shapeless mass.

H. H. FURNESS, JR., '88.

THE VIRGIN PRAIRIE

A SILENT sea of solid swells and crests,
   Across whose barren wastes the flight of time
   Has passed with noiseless wings, and left no sign
Of human habitation; no bequests
   Of beauty, culture, art, or native grace.
This swelling ridge of earth on which I stand, —
A single wave of one vast rolling land,
   That meets my gaze where'er I turn my face.
A soundless, treeless wilderness: it seems
   Fresh from the hand of God, without the stain
   Of human sin and suffering and shame, —
A land of future promise and of dreams.
   Now, like mid-ocean, it appears to me
   Only a type of God's immensity.

                         HARRISON J. HOLT, '98.

WIND VOICES

THE wind comes roaring, roaring, love,
  Across the bay and river;
Before its chilling blasts, I see
  The oak-trees bend and shiver.
Then bind me closer with thy love,
  And weave thy bonds the stronger,
Lest o'er the stormy, wintry sea
  Thy love again should wander.

I mind me of a Northern land,
  The sturdy ship that bore me,
The wondrous ways, the unknown shores,
  That opened out before me.
I mind me of the raging storm,
  The terror of the sea,
The precious treasure of thy love,
  That bound my heart to thee.

List, how the wind is roaring, love;
  On high the gulls are flying.
List, how the sea is growling, love;
  The winter day is dying.

Then bind me closer with thy love,
   And hold me ever nearer.
Dear is the voice of winter winds;
   Thy love, sweet heart, is dearer.

S. C. BRACKETT, '91.

WATER–LILIES

SOFTLY under bending willows,
  Mirrored in the stream below,
I will float with silent paddle
  Down to where the lilies blow.

Softest breezes stir the willows;
  Whisper all the rushes there,
" Nowhere else on lake or streamlet
  Grow the lilies half so fair.

" Once there came the old king's daughter
  Plucking lilies in this place;
Never in her father's castle
  Afterwards was seen her face.

" We, the secret-whispering rushes,
  Know that she forever dwells
With the nixies of the water,
  Bound forever in their spells.

" In the lilies' golden petals
   You may see her floating hair,
And her breath comes through the water
   When the lilies scent the air."

EBERLY HUTCHINSON, '95.

THE SINGER

UPON the world's averted ear,
  You say, all music falls amiss
Except discordant clink of gold:
  Dead are Shaksperian harmonies;
The finer Grecian sense is lost,
  And all our thoughts are dull and cold.
  You sit with silent voice and hold
In careless hand your silent lute.
  Because, forsooth, the world is deaf
Think you the singer must be mute?
  For shame! take up your lute and sing;
  The voice repays the trembling string.
A hundred thousand listening ears
  Could add no sweetness to your song;
Its tone lies not with him who hears,
  Nor is the careless-seeming world
So wholly deaf; no lofty strain
  Was ever yet entirely lost,
No sweet note ever struck in vain.

ROBERT HIGGINSON FULLER, '88.

RIZPAH

SHE loved them, her dead sons, her fallen pair:
   She spread her sackcloth on the naked rock,
   And she sat by them, mindless of the shock
Of summer heat; and kept the birds of air
Afar by day, and all the night her care
   To chase away the hungry, gnawing flock
   Of prowling beasts. And who would wish to
     mock
At Rizpah as she watched them rotting there?
She watched because she loved them even then.
   And is there one spreads not his robe of sorrow
   Upon the rock where death in life begins,
By his dead deeds? We watch, O sons of men,
   To stay the teeth of Time one more to-morrow
   From rotting, but belov'd, dead sons or sins.

LOUIS HOW, '95.

DREAMS

LEAVE me my dreams. Let others wake and
    weep
To toil with fruit or folly, and to heap
    Vain hours with striving for what shall not be.
Theirs, love — and tears, and life— and sometime
    sleep.
        My dreams for me.

Leave me my dreams. The rest of shadowy hills,
The lull of winds, the warmth that floods and fills
    The scented silence of the noontide bowers,
The rippling symphony of birds and rills
        In sunlit hours.

Leave me my dreams. Warm lips that grow not
    cold,
Soft eyes unaging, hair of fadeless gold,
    Strong love unchanging with the altering years,
Made sweet with myriad kisses many-fold,
        Unwet with tears.

6

Leave me my dreams. High lives and hopes
     unslain,
A little fruit unruined of the rain,
   A little love to brighten hours that be
And blind the aching, passionate eyes of pain.
     My dreams for me.

HERBERT BATES, '90.

IN THE MIST

OVER us both the mist fell fast;
   Afar the bells were ringing;
And the sound of the surf came floating past
Over the ocean deep and vast,
   Like the voice of a mermaid singing.

Over the ocean vast and deep
   Ghost-like the shades came flying;
With dreamy eyes we watched them sweep;
And the world seemed lulled to a gentle sleep
   While the wind and the waves were sighing.

Onward we rocked like a phantom ship,
   Thoughtlessly, dreamily sailing;
Watching our anchor rise, and dip
Into the surge with its armored tip
   As the light of the day was paling.

A single gull with silvery breast
   Like a sprite by the clouds was roaming,
And through the mist in the white-robed west,
With one pale star in her nether crest,
   The moon peered into the gloaming.

The pale new moon hung in the sky,
A halo round her glowing;
And still we floated gently by,
Hearing the waters moan and sigh,
Restlessly, fitfully flowing.

PERCY LOUIS SHAW, '97.

THE NOBLER LIGHT

WITH all the soul within me and suppressed
Before the sunset, heard I, and confessed,
A breath of God from out the whispered hand
Held o'er the lips of the great speaking west.

Heard it and all the soul within me burned;
Heard it and wondered at the secret learned;
And all the busy accidents of life
Have taken it, and it has ne'er returned.

So once to every serf and every king
Wide open do the doors of heaven swing:
He will not enter; but the choice is his
To see a nobler light on everything.

P. H. SAVAGE, '93.

A FUTURE RETROSPECT

WHEN all the world is cold, dear heart,
  And all the skies are furled,
We two shall look from heaven's own gate
  Down on the empty world.
Dear heart, the sorrow and the pain
  Shall never grieve us then;
And we shall smile as we look down,
  Half weep, then smile again.

Our thoughts shall such soft pathos have
  As when a man shall come,
From wandering of many years,
  Back to a silent home, —
Like sunshine on a vacant hearth,
  And ashes gray and cold,
And ghostly squares upon the wall
  Where portraits were of old.

ROBERT PALFREY UTTER, '98.

THE BURIAL OF ALARIC

'T IS night; 'tis night. The pale moonlight,
  How fitfully it gleams;
The willows nod; the golden-rod,
O'ercome with sleep, droops toward the sod
  In vague and restless dreams.

And to the skies, the river sighs
  With sad and dreary note;
And on its breast the golden stars
Seem changed to long and brilliant bars
  That idly rock and float.

Say canst thou hear, afar, anear,
  The tramp of armèd men?
And canst thou hear the bugle's call,
Its trembling echoes rise and fall,
  Till all grows still again?

Busentum's tide, though swift and wide,
  Turned from its course must be;

Through other fields its waves must pour
Adown the long and sandy shore
   Into the silent sea.

A tomb, a tomb in dark and gloom
   Beneath the river bed,
They make for him, their proudest boast
Who led their wild and varied host.
   King Alaric is dead.

Ten thousand slaves with heavy breath
   His lonely grave prepare.
In dismal tone the waters moan;
A gull sails by, alone, alone
   Upon the midnight air.

The task is done ere morning sun;
   With slow and measured tread
They bear him on, nor tear, nor sound;
With spearheads turnèd toward the ground
   In honor to the dead.

They lay him low; the moon's bright glow
   Fades down into the West;
The furious waves roll back again.
They kill the slaves; and sadly then
   They leave him to his rest.

'T is morn; 't is morn.   How drearily
  The restless breezes moan!
The waters whisper o'er his head:
"The king, the king, the king is dead,
  His sepulchre unknown."

PERCY LOUIS SHAW, '97.

ATTAINMENT

THROUGH my open window comes the sweet
    perfuming
   Of roses reddening under skies of June;
   No sight more fair than roses in red bloom,
   No air more sweet than doth the rose perfume;
And yet was never there a rose but died in
    blooming.

ALGERNON TASSIN, '92.

THE SONG OF THE SEA-SHELL

THROUGH the long ages of infinite sadness
  All of thy song is a still endless sigh.
Hast thou, then, never known aught of life's
    gladness?
  Canst thou not breathe me one joyous reply?

Tell me, thou thing from the depths of the ocean,
  Tell me the beauties hid under the wave, —
Sea grasses moving in rhythmical motion,
  Cool gliding currents — Nay, mute as the
    grave,

Save for the song that thou ever art singing,
  Save for the breathings that ever reply,
Deep melancholy in sweet numbers bringing,
  Song of the ocean that lives in a sigh.

Through these long ages of infinite sadness
  All of thy song is a still endless sigh;
Never an accent of all of life's gladness,
  Never aught else than thy mournful reply.

                              JOHN R. CORBIN, '92.

LOVE AND THE VIOLETS

WHAT is it, Love, lives in the violet,
Or rose, or laurestine, that makes each fair?
Did thy soul, journeying, once linger there
Among those petals?   Was thy soft heart set
To pulsate in those changeful, nameless hues?
Did thy breath lend them fragrance, thy quick
    sighs
Wet their reproachless, sympathetic eyes;
Thy thoughts, as guiltless then, those brows
    suffuse?
Yes, so it is; Thou madest all their worth,
Thus blessing even as Thou blessest now
Through human benediction.   Here, beside
The way, I find Thee, and wherever Earth
Holds beauty up to Heaven, there, I vow,
All fairness doth of thy love's grace reside.

TREADWELL CLEVELAND, JR., '96.

THE DEPARTURE

THE skies are cold and hard; the dead lights
     trail
  On the long hills; the bitter day is o'er.
Closer I fold my cloak against the gale;
  For I return no more.

No more! the vow shall not be reconciled;
  How long, how bitter was the day I bore!
Enough! and now away into the wild,
  Away, to turn no more.

Surely I shadowed on the coming days
  Th' embracing trust and love of childish lore;
For now, be it blame I leave behind or praise,
  I may return no more.

On, on!   How long the way, the time how brief!
  Folly to linger round the scene of yore!
Away with memory, and the memory's grief;
  For I return no more.

I ask, can ever this dark night pale to morn,
　And has yon dubious morrow aught in
　　store?
Or shall it find me weary and forlorn,
　Who can return no more?

If then the night grow blacker with black
　cloud,
　And sink the road to nothingness before;
If break the heart; still should I say, "I
　vowed,
　And shall return no more"?

If then I madden, if I yield, and yearn
　For such past light as once the evening
　　wore;
And if it come to *death* or to return,
　Still shall I turn no more?

Some voice shall guide me in the night that
　falls,
　Assure that I shall reach the further shore,
And nerve the failing heart, while still it
　calls,
　"On! for thou turnest no more."

Then on! Not much avails the will, the thought;
  Abandonment the voice of reason swore.
What recks it, then? The mould of Fate is
    wrought;
  And, lo! I turn no more.

JOSEPH TRUMBULL STICKNEY, '95.

MORN

I LOVE to walk against the yellow light,
The lemon yellow of the first daylight,
When clear and cold above the frozen earth
    The white sun rises far down to the right.

And then to think of life is very sweet;
The shackles fall and drop about one's feet;
And in the clear forgetfulness of morn
    It seems the world and life are all complete.

'T is good to be forgotten and forget;
To look upon the sun and so beget
A golden present and a past that's free,
    A little time of memory and regret.

And when one strikes and stumbles on a stone,
And turns to find the wingèd fancies flown,
Yet through the passages of life that day
    Will run a radiance other than its own.

P. H. SAVAGE, '93.

WORTH

I

I DREAMT about the temples of old time,
  The gray, tremendous pyramids, the towns
Of nations fallen from their mighty prime,
  The melancholy sphinx that lonely frowns
  Upon the quiet, stretching sand that drowns
A people deep as doth the Dead Sea's slime,
  The works whereat the races and the crowns
Of old have wrought with toil and craft and
    crime.

And dreaming thus, I knew the lot of man,
  His paltriness and mould'ring multitude,
His life, its vanity and little span,
How all his grandest works are but the food
  Of time; then heard I mournful whisperings
  Of an eternal tragedy of things.

II

I saw the old white moon above the trees
  That shone on Adam in his paradise,
  That shines on the everlasting rise
And fall of realms and races, lands and seas,

7

That every little child has wailed to win,
Whither both saint and sinner turn their sight,
Feeling beneath its purity of light
　　Their universal brotherhood of sin.

I saw the aged moon, whose frosty face
　　Shines softly on the noble and the vile,
　　The comic and the gentle and the grim,
The tragic and the dingy common-place,
　　With just the faintest wrinkle of a smile
　　Traced in the shadows of its lower rim.

Henry B. Eddy, '94.

VENUS AT TWILIGHT

THROUGH vistas soft the sunset light
    Is shining faint and low;
Above the rose-clouds, changing white, '
Venus, the herald of the night,
    Begins to glow.

O fairest light of twilight skies!
    Thy beauty, flaming far,
Burns brighter as the bright day dies,
Lightening the dusk that round thee lies,
    Love's guardian star.

Thy orb, above the falling day
    Hung like a spark of fire,
'Twixt light and darkness set midway,
Shines with a clear unfaltering ray
    Of Love's desire.

Lower must thy fair light decline,
    In loveliness to set;
To rise on other lands and shine,
Greeted by other songs than mine,
    Eternal yet.

J. H. BOYNTON, '90.

ADRIFT

THE sun is down; my spirit drifts
    Afar to the isles of sleep,
Where dim, forgotten mem'ries pass,
As shadows through the meadow-grass
    Away o'er the drowsy deep.

I hear the sound of dripping oars,
    Beyond in the red-rimmed west;
A phantom crew is by my side;
Their rhythmic song steals down the tide,
    To die in a sea of rest.

Grand melody in sweetest tones
    That blend with the charmèd stream,
Until the waters cease to flow;
The zephyr bows and whispers low;
    I doze in a fancied dream.

Asleep in life, asleep in death, —
    Ah, death has the keener knife.

Go, mortal, blunt its sharpest blade
With stones of faith thy God has made:
   They lie at the gate of life.

The sun is down; my spirit drifts
   Afar to the isles of sleep,
Where dim, forgotten mem'ries pass,
As shadows through the meadow-grass,
   Away o'er the drowsy deep.

M. F. CARNEY, '96.

THE LOVER AND THE DEAD

" YOU bide beyond all mortal years;
    Yet if I pray and weep,
May one not break the barriers
    That fast your presence keep?"

The Dead feel not the living tears
    Nor end their endless sleep.

" O Lady, in some lonesome lane
    I oft will quickly start
And think I see you once again,
    Belovèd of my heart."

You turn to find but shifting rain
    That drives the boughs apart.

" But all the circling days we knew
    So with this day inweaves
It seems the very voice of you
    In every covert grieves."

'T is but the autumn winds that rue
    The dying of the leaves.

JOHN MACK, JR., '95.

THE LITANY OF BATTLES

THE cloud of war turns day to night;
The beacons flare to left, to right;
Heroes lead hero hosts to fight.
    God save us in the pain of death.

Now men atone for guilt with guilt,
Tear down the temples they have built,
Spill blood for wine already spilt.
    God save us in the sins of death.

We know not if we rise or fall;
We know not why the trumpets call;
God, make us know thou rulest all.
    God save us in the fear of death.

If we be brothers bound from birth,
Or foemen from an alien earth,
God judge us lastly worth for worth.
    God save us in the chance of death.

If there be war beyond the grave,
If warrior hands shall grasp the glaive,
Shall heroes here be Heaven's brave?
   God save us in the doubt of death.

Straight past the battle dragon's jaw,
Hard fighting up the path of law,
We scale the heights our fathers saw.
   God save us in the joy of death.

JOHN ALBERT MACY, '99.

HESPERUS

Now night is come.   Aloft the western sky
The evening star in regal splendor shines.
Deep in the bosom of the quiet sea,
Fitful, uncertain, roaming here and there,
Most like the phantom of an unsphered star,
Her image bears her ghost-like company.
And when the night-wind springs from out the
        west,
Moving along its rippling path apace,
Yonder deep-floating star is quickly caught,
And shivered to a thousand glittering gems
To strew the unknown caverns of the sea.

JOHN R. CORBIN, '92.

A FACE

So you are often restless, and you yearn,
And oft have doubts.   You are not always sure
That life is worth much, or that to endure
For joys all fleeting, wounds that ever burn,
Is profitable.   Disillusioned, stern,
Play on your part with manner all demure,
Smile when you should, and keep that fair face
     pure
From any trace of love or love's return.
But I prefer — perversely, as I know, —
To keep my old illusions, and I dare
Think men still human, women part divine,
For untaught me, love's roses ever blow;
Still live strong, wholesome friendships, every-
     where;
And slowly life grows old and rich, — like wine.

BARTLETT BROOKS, 1900.

DRIFTING

DRIFTING in our frail canoe
  On the dusky, silent stream,
  Dearest, see! The sunset-gleam
Fires love's torch for me and you.

Coral clouds and pearly sky,
  Flaming in the farthest west,
  Softly whisper peace and rest,
Peace and rest that never die.

Let us shun the sable shore,
  Frowning at us slipping by.
  Let's be happy, you and I,
Drifting, drifting evermore.

                    H. H. CHAMBERLIN, JR., '95.

WHITHER?

AGNES, thou child of harmony, now fled
  From scenes once bright-illumined with thy
    smile,
  So innocent and kind, free from the guile
Of Orient charm, mysterious and dread, —
Where shall I seek thee, maid? Thou art not
    dead.
  No, Nature's heart would break, count all else
    vile,
  Bereft of thee e'en for a little while.
Where art thou, then? Hast to the violet sped
  That with its gentle blue bespeaks thine eye?
    To rippling stream, the echo of thy voice?
    To wooing wind that, kissing, says ' Rejoice ! '
  Or to the rose-bush with its fainting sigh,
' Ah ! too lovely for a season long ! ' —
Or, art thou on fair angel lips a song?

                       PHILIP BECKER GOETZ, '93.

SHAKSPERE

NO marvels now can startle my belief:
   Tell me of gods that scale the peaks of heaven
To scan the future for the world's relief;
   Of Titans old, whose grizzled locks are riven
By the cold-cutting North; of wanded elves
   That light their lanterns by the evening star;
Of hunchèd dwarfs, whose toil the mountain
     delves, —
   Tell of all these, and I shall vow they are.
Or speak of miracles, and I shall say
   Blind eyes may drink the rainbow, halting
     limbs
Outfoot fleet Mercury, and ears of clay
   Thrill in delight at sound of seraph hymns.
All wonders now have my credulity
Since — wondrous Shakspere — I believe in thee.

Percy Wallace MacKaye, '97.

LOVE SONG

Dear Love, I would not for the world
  That you were other than you are;
Far rather let the sky be furled
  And quenched each sun and star.

Your tears for me have left their trace,
  And care its record plain to see:
Not one of these would I efface,
  For each is dear to me.   .

Dear Love, I pray to God with tears
  You will be ever as you are.'
For you have been, through all the years,
  My north and guiding star.

J. F. Brice, '99.

MENOETES

WHO is this fellow floundering in the wave,
  Flung from the Trojan galley thundering by?
  Lightly, my friend; he may be you, or I!
This passage from the master to the slave
Is but a flash: the pinnacle we crave
  Totters and falls; and life is but to fly
  The dark immediate anguish surging nigh,
To foil the shrewd enclosure of the grave.
So, when I read of old Menoetes overthrown
  By raging Gyas to the furrowed brine,
I cannot wholly laugh: there is a tone
  Of merry sadness in the poet's line
  That tells me summer suns will never shine
When skies with tyrannous clouds are overblown.

E. A. ROBINSON, Sp.

SUNSET

THE sweet, low lisping of the sunset's breath
   Ripples the water in a silver strand.
   Apollo reins awhile his chariot band
Ere the bright glory meets its daily death.
The woods bow down to what the ripple saith
    That beats upon the broad, bare, barren sand,
    Surging sweet sorrows of the night at hand,
Within whose arms the pale moon blossometh.
We stood together; from thy childish breast
   I heard a sighing for the day now dead;
Within mine arms I felt thy body rest
   And saw the glow lie blessing round thy head,
As if the sun had also loved thee best,
   And o'er thy face his latest beauty shed.

ANONYMOUS.

ARABIA

ACROSS the hills, beyond the sea,
  The pale moon shines on crystal streams;
There comes no sound from lawn or lea;
No voice to set the echoes free
  And break the spell of aimless dreams.

Hast thou not said, " I love repose,
  Where thought unhindered comes to me,
Where fancy blooms unchecked and grows
Fed by a fire that gleams and glows
  Like sunlight on a depthless sea "?

Here when the morning lilies rise,
  And crimson dawn leaps into noon;
Here shalt thou rest thy weary eyes,
Hid from the glare of burning skies,
  And cradled by a quiet tune.

But if at morn or eventide
  Some idle vision claims the hour,

8

Pray throw its empty spell aside
As thou wouldst scatter far and wide
   The petals of a faded flower.

Think then of me for one short space,
   Who dream of thee each passing day.
I beg thee for a moment's grace,
And in thy heart a resting-place,
   That I be near, though far away.

PERCY LOUIS SHAW, '97.

TO BEAUTY

SHOULD heaven draw thee to her fair domain,
  And death dissolve thy form in common air,
  And turn to mortal breath thy uttered prayer,
Thy beauties all invisible remain,
As shall thy goodness live on earth again;
  Though they to that ethereal 'bode may rise,
  Here echo memories of thy lost replies,
The blessings that in weary hearts are lain;
For Beauty ne'er hath limned a fairer face,
  Nor Goodness e'er illumed a brighter eye,
And surely He who is the Lord of Grace
  Will never let such Truth and Beauty die.
What though they change their mortal dwelling-
    place,
  Their charms shall still survive beneath the sky.

WALTER LITTLEFIELD, Sp.

GREATNESS

LONG through the crumbling ages there has
   passed
  To many men an honor over great;
  Their history is read but in the fate
Of time which followed; not in that which cast
Its shadow darkly downward on the massed
 - Assembly of their deeds, to hide the state
  Of man and darken to our view the weight
Of virtue and of vice which could not last.
Talk not of famous men whose warlike lives
  A load of Stygian woe upon mankind
Have garnered, but thank God there still survives
  The work of men so truly great, that find
Whatever fault he will, not one who thrives
  By knowledge will deny th' Eternal Mind.

EDWIN FRANCIS EDGETT, '94.

AN OLD SONG NEW–SUNG

OH! the wind comes moaning over the sea,
  And the wind moans over the land.
When will my ship come back to me,
  As I wearily wait on the sand?

I sent her forth as the daylight dawned,
  And my heart's love speeded her sail;
My smile was bright and my hope was strong,
  As I prayed for a favoring gale.

Oh! the sun rose higher over the sea,
  And the tide ebbed out from the land,
And my smile was bright and my hope was strong,
  As I waited and walked the strand.

The water danced in the full noon's ray,
  And my heart it danced in tune,
For my ship would come at the set of sun
  And her sail with the rising moon.

The sun blushed out from the bank of cloud,
    With his cheek 'gainst the ocean's face,
And my hope grew strong as the moon came on
    In ripples of silvery lace.

But the stars sank down far off in the east,
    And the stars sank down in the west,
And my smile was sad and my hope was faint,
    As I waited in vague unrest.

And the morning flaunts his red in the sky,
    And the waves, they laugh in their glee;
But my smile is gone and my hope is dead,
    As I wait all alone by the sea.

And so I watch and wait by day,
    And I watch and wait by night,
And when it is day, "in the evening," I say,
    And at eve, "with the dawning light."

But the wind comes moaning over the sea,
    And the wind moans over the land.
When will my ship come back to me
    As I wearily wait on the sand?

ALGERNON TASSIN, '92.

OLD YUCATAN

OLD Yucatan! where shod foot never fell,
  Slowly I break my way and silently.
    Quiet is genius of each fern, each tree,
Each dreaming stream, each slowly oozing well.
Quiet and brazen sun which seem to tell
  Of some old, speechless, tiptoe mystery
    Bid me be still and cease my inquiry, —
Lure me to seek the secret of the spell.
Lo, a hushed empire, stone yet firm on stone,
  Pyramid-stepped in sky-ascending shrines;
    Palaces, temples, places, paven ways;
Solidly graven walls which, without tone,
  Speak each a strange, hard speech in square-
    cut lines;
    Carved Maya faces, gazing as you gaze.

              J. F. BRICE, '99.

THE CATHEDRAL

HALF forgotten echoes wake,
Dusty, cobwebbed corners shake,
As the Münster chime-bells take
   Their vespered tolling.

Groups of bashful maidens fair
Fill the twilight-shadowed square;
Ling'ring yet, they climb the stair
   To their devotions.

High above the priestly drone,
Lifts the fairest maid, alone;
Crimson-hued her robe of stone,
   The sunlight's plaything.

Frozen work of vanished hands,
Lost in evening prayer she stands,
Her reeking censers, perfumed lands,
   The world, her altar.

Homeward-circling pigeons rest,
Gems upon her sunset crest,
Bearing from the fading west
    God's benediction.

Wan her laces grow and cold,
As the sun steals back its gold;
Another day her life has told
    With this fair even.

E. L. DUDLEY, 1900.

THE HAVEN

TWO mighty arms of land shut out the wide
  Mad flood, and shelter in their cosey lee
  The buoyant ships that totter lazily
On the slow-breathing bosom of the tide;
Calm in the bay the beaten vessels ride;
  Safe from the storms that churn the deep, deep
    sea,
  The weary mariner is resting free,
Deaf to the baffled fiend that roars outside.

Safe from the blustering hurricane we two
  Shall anchor in the harbor love has made.
  The shore will murmur with the serenade
Of little waves that dance in from the blue.
Though the dark sea may beat the long night
    through,
  Love, little love, we shall not be afraid.

JOHN ALBERT MACY, '99.

ART

BUILD thee an altar in thy inmost heart
  And sacrifice thereon meek-eyed content:
Born of the blaze of all thou hast, shall start
  Upon thy sight a dream-starred firmament.

PHILIP BECKER GOETZ, '93.

THE BUILDER — SCIENCE

I SAW in outline on the northern skies
  A fair-haired giant, building, with his hands,
  And lifting rock on rock; and now expands
The growing structure. Skilful, ay, and wise,
He shapes and plans, and wearies as he tries
  To fit the mighty work to those demands
  His laboring brain requires; till now there
    stands
A towered temple complete before his eyes.
  He rests, and lies beside a running brook,
  And in its voice grows thoughtful; then in pain
He starts, and knows the birth of the divine.
  Touched with the dreadful question of that look,
  I turned away, but saw him once again
Dead, lying where he should have built his
    shrine.

                        P. H. SAVAGE, '93.

CANOE SONG

Dip! Dip! Softly slip
  Down the river shining wide.
Dim and far the dark banks are;
  Life is love and naught beside,
  Onward drifting with the tide.

. Drip, drip, from paddle-tip
  Myriad ripples swirl and swoon;
Shiv'ring 'mid the ruddy stars,
  Mirrored in the deep lagoon,
  Faintly floats the mummied moon.

Soft, soft, high aloft,
  Ever thus till time is done,
Worlds will die; may thou and I
  Glide beneath a gentler sun,
  Young as now and ever one.

                    E. Frère Champney, '96.

LIFE HOPES

THE waves are breaking on the outer bar,
   Never to reach the long-desirèd goal.
Out in the offing, where the sea-gulls are,
The waves are breaking on the outer bar,
Swelling so proudly in from seaward far,
   And dashed to foam upon the unseen shoal.
The waves are breaking on the outer bar,
   Never to reach the long-desirèd goal.

                         ANONYMOUS.

NOVISSIMUM VERBUM

I

Bolt fast the door.   The past that lies behind
  That studded portal must not live again;
  Pleasure was there and throbbing hours of pain,
Success, disaster, hope, and fear born blind.
And yet, in spite of wasted days, resigned
  Ambitions, dreams, and struggles that were vain,
  All is not lost, for memories remain,
And memory was ever over-kind.
And still we know God's blessed messenger,
  The Future, holds all promises in store;
With strength loss-fostered let us follow her;
  Let here, as at Araunah's threshing-floor,
Whatever plague endures be stayed with myrrh
  And incense of high aims.   Bolt fast the door.

II

Go forth and fear not; strike, attack, defend;
  In thine invulnerable self stand sure;
  Self-armed and self-defended, self-secure,
Victor, thou all shalt to thy purpose bend.

Ay, victor if the enemy shall send
    Their deadliest darts into thy bosom pure;
    Victor if captive spite of every lure,
Falling in harness, fighting to the end.
The stars and all the heavens above us fill
    With one Te Deum unto self; the lord
Of self of destiny is king; so still
    Fight the good fight, however weak the sword,
With single purpose and unconquered will,
    One aim, one hope, one struggle, one reward.

REGINALD WRIGHT KAUFFMAN, Sp.

PRÆTERITA

THE world has quite outgrown her song
Because the world has sung too long;
And so the world shall sing no more,
And song is o'er.

For men are wiser than of old,
And men have learnt the worth of gold,
And men have set their hearts above
The spell of love.

Men's eyes shall cease to weep, they say,
For pity in the coming day,
And none shall laugh through all the earth
Made bare of mirth.

Then Heaven that we hoped, shall be
As the old tale of Arcady,
And man, in spirit as in breath,
Shall die in death.

9

The world has quite outgrown her song,
Because the world has sung too long;
And so the world shall sing no more,
And song is o'er.

HERBERT BATES, '90.

Part II

Class-Day Odes

DEAR Mother, we turn from thy beautiful
   throne
  On the fair, watered slopes of the west,
To wander and struggle, unguided, alone,
  Till Night in the path bars our quest.
Thou hast given us strength from thy bountiful
   heart
  That will keep us through tempest and sun:
Each glance at thy face, and each thought what
   thou art
  Shall herald a victory won.

The mirage of the future gleams temptingly
   bright,
  And quickens our steps to the fore:
We shall feel, though we stay not, thy motherly
   sight
  Still blessing our path as of yore.

At dusk, when we turn, and in memory rove
   On the ways that are dark'ning towards thee,
May the afterglow brighten the summits we love,
   Thy forehead our Hesperus be.

ROBERT ELKIN NEIL DODGE, '89.

FAIR Harvard, ere we in our turn pass away
  From thy portals, our song we upraise, —
One note in the song of the world-sundered
    throng
  Of thy sons, who are one in thy praise;
From thy throne by the storm-beaten shores of
    the east
  To the western far shores of the sea,
That thy splendor and fame may endure, and thy
    name
  In the mouths of thy sons yet to be.

Through the change of the years wherein laughter
    and tears
  Shall be mingled as sunshine and shade,
We shall march with thy grace for our guidance,
    thy face
  Still before us, by dread undismayed.

As the thunder and song of the sea on the long
  Sea-ramparts, thy praise shall ascend;
And to thee, who give might to thy sons in the
    light
  Of thy learning, be fame without end.

HERBERT BATES, '90.

FAIR Harvard, the years that have wearied thy
   sons
  Have but added new glory to thee ;
For thy course is as sure as the river that runs
  Through thine own level plains to the sea ;
With the strength of the age, as the ages in-
   crease,
  Thou growest more firm and secure ;
By thy watchword of truth to high blessings of
   peace
  Ever onward, while time doth endure.

We are youngest and least of the band of thy
   sons,
  With no laurels to bend for thy brow,
No glorious names, like the long-parted ones
  Whose mighty deeds honor thee now ;
Yet the lessons we learned are the same that they
   knew,

We have walked in the ways that they trod,
And our hearts like the hearts of thy heroes are
    true
To thine honor, our country, our God.

                        SEWELL CARROLL BRACKETT, '91.

Fair Mother, we pray for thy help ere we
    turn
  Toward the doubt and the darkness ahead;
May the fires of thy beacons flash high as they
    burn
  And illumine the path where we tread;
May their brilliance extend with the growth of thy
    fame
    Through the wastes of the outer world's
    night,
Till our doubt disappear before faith in thy
    name
  And our darkness give place to thy light.

So our strength shall increase in the struggle with
    life
  For the reward from the future's slow hand,
And our hearts, in return for thine aid in the
    strife,
  Be as one in thy grace through the land,

Till the hosts of thy sons from the south and the
    north
    And the wide parted shores of the sea,
Shall transmute each success which the years may
    bring forth
    Into glory, fair Harvard, for thee.

SAMUEL PITTS DUFFIELD, '92.

F AIR Harvard, how fairer than childhood's fond
     dream
   Dost thou shine in our treasure to-day!
We have known thee, and loved thee, and memories
     teem
   Ever sweet with the notes of thy lay.
But the chord of our parting is trembling and
     low,
   As it echoes the soul's deep refrain;
And we stay, while it kindles in love's crescent
     glow,
   For the blessings that hallow its strain.

Breathe thy beautiful soul o'er the dew of our
     youth,
   When we wander from learning's fair halls;
And soft be the years to the whispers of
     truth
   As the ivy that clings on the walls.

O shrine of the pure! in praise and in wrath
  Join thy living in sacred accord;
And the faith of thy dead shall illumine the path
  To the heights of the vision of God.

DAVID SAVILLE MUZZEY, '93.

FIERCE maiden, true life, whom we wooed
  with grim fight,
  In past dreams to thy conquest we woke.
To thee, fire-encircled, asleep on thy height,
  Through the flame, with love-wakening, we
  broke.
With thee, then, for honor we sought in our
  pride,
  Still heroes in good and in sin;
But now our dream fades, and earth's truth, our
  new guide,
  Into mists melts the glory we'd win.

Sweet maiden, true life, now with reverent
  love,
  In truth's light to thy conquest we wake;
Thy sleep on the rock, with the red blaze
  above,
  Through the flame, with love-wakening, we
  break.

Now for thee may we live in thy power supreme,
    For thee to brave evil and fear;
And when we awake to find earth but a dream,
    In God's truth may we find thee still near.

HENRY COPLEY GREENE, '94.

Across storm-driven spaces, our Lady of
    Truth,
    We beheld thee fair shining in grace,
And rapt by the charm of thy radiant youth,
    We toiled for a glimpse of thy face.
In darkness and doubt thy smile was our light,
    As we looked, from deep places, to thee;
Though shaken by error, yet strong with thy
    might,
    We fought for the truth that makes free.

To win thee, our Lady, in days that are past,
    With stress in fierce conflict we wrought,
Yet, because of thy fairness, we reck not the cost,
    For thou art the guerdon we sought.
Through evil and good, with thee at our side,
    Triumphant we pass on life's road;
Up heights of achievement wilt thou be our guide,
    Till we stand in the presence of God.

CARLETON ELDREDGE NOYES, '95.

In thy temple, dear Mother, our last song we
    raise
    Of honor and praise to thy name,
Who hast given us our armor, and girded us well,
    For life's struggle for glory and fame.
And sadly we leave this dear home of our souls,
    Where truth's banner stands ever unfurled,
Where on altars of faith burns the incense of hope
    That shall cheer and inspire the world.

Yet e'er to thy shrines we in spirit may turn,
    Though far from thy temple we roam,
For thy sympathy wide as the world spreads
    abroad,
    And in every land findeth a home.
Where'er truth is worshipped and error despised,
    Where'er freedom lifts her fair brow,
Where'er passion is scorned, and the spirit obeyed,
    There ever, dear Harvard, art thou.

GEORGE HENRY CHASE, '96.

Loving Mother, the spell of thy beauty this
    day
  Hath the souls of thy children bound fast;
Thy glory serene spreadeth sunshine and joy
  O'er this festival, dearest and last.
Yet sudden and still as the passing of clouds
  Come swift shadows that deepen and grow,
When, thy sweet lips a-tremble, thy cheeks wet
    with tears,
  Thy last blessing thou giv'st, ere we go.

Yet linger we would not: thy lesson is learned;
  'T is time not to dream, but to do!
Like our pale hero-brothers, to smite down the
    wrong,
  And to thee, fairest Mother, be true.
Farewell! yet we know that thine eyes follow far
  Over battle-slope dim and dark sea;
Thy blessing hath armed us, the toil and the pain
  To bear bravely, for God and for thee.

              ·   JAMES EDGAR GREGG, '97.

WE have slept till the morn in thy chambers
    of peace,
  (And the dream was the vision of youth!)
At the dawn of the day we arise and go forth
  In the armor and shield of the Truth.
By the Beautiful Gate, ere the shadowy vale
  Shall receive us, we bow down the knee,
And we lift in the light of the morning our hymn
  To the glory, fair Harvard, of thee!

In the wilderness born, through the wilderness
    still
  Thou preparest the way of the Lord,
Till the nations are one in the sound of a Name
  And the ploughshare supplanteth the sword;
Till, crowned with the crown of the victory won,
  Thou shalt hearken, o'er land and o'er sea,
The song of thanksgiving at eventide raised
  To the glory of God and of Thee!

FULLERTON LEONARD WALDO, '98.

Index of Authors

Index of Authors

www.ingramcontent.com/pod-product-compliance
Lightning Source LLC
Chambersburg PA
CBHW021123020726
47500CB00003B/904